DATE DUE

JUL - - 2004

Tools

Search

Notes

Discuss

▶ MyReportLinks.com Books

Go!

U.S. WARS

THE VIETNAM WAR

A MyReportLinks.com Book

Carl R. Green

MyReportLinks.com Books

an imprint of

Enslow Publishers, Inc.

Box 398, 40 Industrial Road
Berkeley Heights, NJ 07922
USA

MyReportLinks.com Books, an imprint of Enslow Publishers, Inc. MyReportLinks is a trademark of Enslow Publishers, Inc.

Library of Congress Cataloging-in-Publication Data

Green, Carl R.
 The Vietnam War / Carl R. Green.
   v. cm. — (U.S. wars)
Includes bibliographical references and index.
Contents: The Tonkin Gulf Incident — The road to war — A growing commitment, 1954–1961 — The war heats up, 1962–1965 — The turning point, 1966–1970 — Wrapping it up, 1971–1975.
  ISBN 0-7660-5147-1
 1. Vietnamese Conflict, 1961–1975—Juvenile literature. 2. Vietnamese Conflict, 1961–1975—United States—Juvenile literature. [1. Vietnamese Conflict, 1961–1975.] I. Title. II. Series.
  DS557.7.G74 2003
  959.704'3—dc21

                            2003008599

Printed in the United States of America

10 9 8 7 6 5 4 3 2 1

To Our Readers:
Through the purchase of this book, you and your library gain access to the Report Links that specifically back up this book.
The Publisher will provide access to the Report Links that back up this book and will keep these Report Links up to date on **www.myreportlinks.com** for three years from the book's first publication date.
We have done our best to make sure all Internet addresses in this book were active and appropriate when we went to press. However, the author and the Publisher have no control over, and assume no liability for, the material available on those Internet sites or on other Web sites they may link to.
The usage of the MyReportLinks.com Books Web site is subject to the terms and conditions stated on the Usage Policy Statement on **www.myreportlinks.com.**
A password may be required to access the Report Links that back up this book. The password is found on the bottom of page 4 of this book.
Any comments or suggestions can be sent by e-mail to comments@myreportlinks.com or to the address on the back cover.

Photo Credits: Another Vietnam, p. 27; Associated Press, p. 18; Bill Ragan/Painet Inc., p. 39; British Broadcasting Corporation © 2002–2003, pp. 32, 41; © Peter Leuhusen 2000–2003, pp. 33, 36; Corbis Corporation, p. 43; Dwight D. Eisenhower Library, p. 25; National Archives and Records Administration, pp. 1; 11, 13, 16, 23, 29, 30, 31, 35; PBS, p. 22; Richard Nixon Library & Birthplace, p. 38.

Cover Photo: National Archives and Records Administration

Cover Description: Helicopters transport men from the field.

Contents

Report Links **4**

Vietnam War Facts **10**

1 **The Tonkin Gulf Incident** **11**

2 **The Road to War** **15**

3 **A Growing Commitment,
1954–1961** **20**

4 **The War Heats Up, 1962–1965** **26**

5 **The Turning Point, 1966–1970** **32**

6 **Wrapping It Up, 1971–1975** **39**

Chapter Notes **45**

Further Reading **47**

Index **48**

MyReportLinks.com Books
Great Books, Great Links, Great for Research!

MyReportLinks.com Books present the information you need to learn about your report subject. In addition, they show you where to go on the Internet for more information. The pre-evaluated Report Links that back up this book are kept up to date on **www.myreportlinks.com**. With the purchase of a MyReportLinks.com Books title, you and your library gain access to the Report Links that specifically back up that book. The Report Links save hours of research time and link to dozens—even hundreds—of Web sites, source documents, and photos related to your report topic.

Please see "To Our Readers" on the Copyright page for important information about this book, the MyReportLinks.com Books Web site, and the Report Links that back up this book.

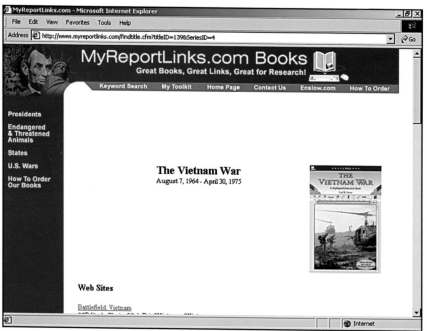

Access:

The Publisher will provide access to the Report Links that back up this book and will try to keep these Report Links up to date on our Web site for three years from the book's first publication date. Please enter **AVW8204** if asked for a password.

▸ The Internet sites described below can be accessed at
http://www.myreportlinks.com

*EDITOR'S CHOICE

▸ Battlefield: Vietnam

At this PBS Web site you can explore the Vietnam War, read a brief history of the war, and view a battlefield time line. You will also learn about guerrilla tactics and the Siege of Khe Sanh.

Link to this Internet site from http://www.myreportlinks.com

*EDITOR'S CHOICE

▸ The Wars for Viet Nam: 1945–1975

From this Vassar College Web site you can examine the Vietnam War from 1945 to 1975. Here you will find an overview of the war, documents and letters, and links to other resources.

Link to this Internet site from http://www.myreportlinks.com

*EDITOR'S CHOICE

▸ Vietnam Online

This PBS Web site provides a comprehensive look at the Vietnam War. Here you will find brief biographies of key players, an extensive time line, essays, photographs, and well-written descriptions of major battles.

Link to this Internet site from http://www.myreportlinks.com

*EDITOR'S CHOICE

▸ The Fall of Saigon

The *New York Times* provides coverage of the Vietnam War with an emphasis on the fall of Saigon. This site includes many articles from the *New York Times* archives dating back to 1966, as well as many photographs and graphics.

Link to this Internet site from http://www.myreportlinks.com

*EDITOR'S CHOICE

▸ Cold War

CNN Interactive Web site provides a series on the Cold War. Here you will find a time line of events that occurred during this time period. Click on "Episode-By-Episode" to learn about the Vietnam War, its protesters, and the outcome of the war.

Link to this Internet site from http://www.myreportlinks.com

*EDITOR'S CHOICE

▸ Maps of the Vietnam War

This Web site presents fourteen different maps from the Vietnam War. These high-resolution maps document the progress of the war from 1954 to 1975.

Link to this Internet site from http://www.myreportlinks.com

Report Links

The Internet sites described below can be accessed at
http://www.myreportlinks.com

▶ **All Weather Attack**

All Weather Attack is dedicated to the role of the A6 Intruder aircraft
in the Vietnam War. Here you will find official and unofficial histories,
photographs, testimonials, a discussion forum, technical details, and more.

Link to this Internet site from http://www.myreportlinks.com

▶ **Another Vietnam**

This Web site, an online companion to the *National Geographic* book
entitled *Another Vietnam: Pictures of the War from the Other Side*, holds
a collection of powerful photographs snapped during the Vietnam War.

Link to this Internet site from http://www.myreportlinks.com

▶ **CIA and the Vietnam Policy Makers: Three Episodes 1962–1968**

This publication, from the Center for Studies of Intelligence, examines events
that occurred during the Vietnam War from 1962 to 1968, including
President Lyndon B. Johnson's decision to "go big" in Vietnam.

Link to this Internet site from http://www.myreportlinks.com

▶ **Cu Chi: The Underground War**

This article, from the BBC Web site, describes the underground tunnels
built by the Vietcong during the Vietnam War. The coverage includes images
and diagrams of the tunnels.

Link to this Internet site from http://www.myreportlinks.com

▶ **Dwight Eisenhower: The Cautious Warrior**

The American Presidency Web site features a comprehensive biography of
Dwight Eisenhower. Click on "Foreign Affairs" to learn about his involvement
in the Vietnam War.

Link to this Internet site from http://www.myreportlinks.com

▶ **Ending the Vietnam War**

On the U.S. Department of State Web site you will find a discussion of
how the Vietnam War was ended. Here you will learn about the role
President Richard Nixon played during the final stages of the conflict.

Link to this Internet site from http://www.myreportlinks.com

 The Internet sites described below can be accessed at
http://www.myreportlinks.com

▶ **Indochina—Vietnam, Cambodia, and Laos**
On the Avalon Project at Yale Law School Web site you will find
documents from the Vietnam War from 1950 to 1964.

Link to this Internet site from http://www.myreportlinks.com

▶ **In Pictures: Fall of Saigon**
You will find images of the fall of Saigon on the BBC News Web site.
You will also find links to other stories related to the Vietnam War.

Link to this Internet site from http://www.myreportlinks.com

▶ **Lyndon B. Johnson: The War on Poverty President**
The American President Web site offers readers a comprehensive
biography of Lyndon B. Johnson's life, political career, and legacy.
Click on "Foreign Policy" to learn about his involvement in the
Vietnam War.

Link to this Internet site from http://www.myreportlinks.com

▶ **Operation Rolling Thunder**
On the Military Analysis Network Web site you will find a brief
description of Operation Rolling Thunder, the bombing campaign
against North Vietnam that began on February 24, 1965.

Link to this Internet site from http://www.myreportlinks.com

▶ **Peter Peterson: Assignment Hanoi**
This PBS Web site explores the background and history surrounding
Peter Peterson's 1997 assignment as the first U.S. ambassador to
Vietnam after the Vietnam War.

Link to this Internet site from http://www.myreportlinks.com

▶ **Pete Seeger Is Born**
America's Story from America's Library, a Library of Congress Web
site, tells the story of the day Pete Seeger was born. Here you will
learn about this famous songwriter's music and how it relates to the
Vietnam War.

Link to this Internet site from http://www.myreportlinks.com

Report Links

The Internet sites described below can be accessed at
http://www.myreportlinks.com

▶Richard Nixon: The Comeback President

The American President Web site offers a comprehensive biography of Richard M. Nixon. Here you will learn about his life before, during, and after his presidency. Click on "Foreign Affairs" to learn about his involvement in the Vietnam War.

Link to this Internet site from http://www.myreportlinks.com

▶The Secret Side of the Tonkin Gulf Incident

From *Naval History Magazine* you can read an article that explores little-known aspects of the Tonkin Gulf Incident.

Link to this Internet site from http://www.myreportlinks.com

▶*Time* 100: Ho Chi Minh

In the *Time* 100 polls, Ho Chi Minh was rated one of the top twenty "Leaders & Revolutionaries" of the twentieth century. Here at the *Time* Web site you can read a brief biography of his life and learn how he earned a spot in this category.

Link to this Internet site from http://www.myreportlinks.com

▶The Tonkin Gulf Incident: 1964

At the Avalon Project at Yale Law School Web site you will find the text of President Lyndon B. Johnson's message to Congress on August 5, 1964. This was the message that led Congress to authorize the use of force in Vietnam.

Link to this Internet site from http://www.myreportlinks.com

▶Vietnam–A Country Study

The Library of Congress Web site holds a comprehensive history of Vietnam, including chapters on the country's history, geography, culture, economy, government, politics, and national security.

Link to this Internet site from http://www.myreportlinks.com

▶Vietnam Passage: The Journey from War to Peace

This PBS Web site provides a comprehensive look at Vietnam before, during, and after the war. You will also find stories from people involved in the war who viewed their experiences from widely differing perspectives.

Link to this Internet site from http://www.myreportlinks.com

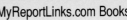
Report Links

The Internet sites described below can be accessed at
http://www.myreportlinks.com

▶**Vietnam: Then and Now**
This ThinkQuest Web site explores the Vietnam War's history from
the past to the present. Here you will learn about the history of the
war, the people involved, and different viewpoints on the war.

Link to this Internet site from http://www.myreportlinks.com

▶**The Vietnam War**
The History Place Web site provides a time line of the United States'
involvement in Vietnam from 1945 to 1975. You can also view a slide
show that features images of war, protesters, and key players.

Link to this Internet site from http://www.myreportlinks.com

▶**The Vietnam War**
You will find a history of the war through images at the Vietnam War
Web site. Each image is accompanied with a brief description of the
photograph. You will also find a time line of the war. *Warning:* Some of
the images on this Web site are quite graphic.

Link to this Internet site from http://www.myreportlinks.com

▶**Vietnam War Poison**
The BBC News Web site presents this article about Agent Orange, a
chemical that was sprayed on fields and forests during the Vietnam War.
You will learn about some children who were exposed to this chemical.

Link to this Internet site from http://www.myreportlinks.com

▶**Vietnam: Yesterday and Today**
The Vietnam: Yesterday and Today Web site provides a time line
of the Vietnam War, beginning in 1930. You will also find a
history of the Vietnam War and a look at Vietnam today.

Link to this Internet site from http://www.myreportlinks.com

▶**The Virtual Wall**
At the Virtual Wall Web site you can take a virtual tour of the names
inscribed on the Vietnam Veterans Memorial wall.

Link to this Internet site from http://www.myreportlinks.com

 Combatants

| United States and the Republic of Vietnam (RVN), with support from Australia, New Zealand, Philippines, South Korea, and Thailand. | Democratic Republic of Vietnam (DRV) and the Vietcong, with support from China and the Soviet Union. |

 Casualties

Note: The following battle casualties are based on the best estimates available, particularly for casualties suffered by the Vietnamese people.[1]

American casualties: 58,202 killed; 304,704 wounded; 2,338 missing in action; 766 POWs.	**North Vietnamese & Vietcong casualties:** 1,100,000 killed; 600,000 wounded during 21 years of war, 1954–75.
South Vietnamese casualties: 223,748 killed; 1,169,763 wounded.	

Total Vietnamese casualties, civilian and military: 2 million dead; 3 million wounded.

A Brief Time Line

1945—Ho Chi Minh proclaims the Democratic Republic of Vietnam.

1954—*May 7:* Ho's Vietminh forces defeat French army at Dien Bien Phu.

   July 21: Geneva Conference divides Vietnam at the 17th parallel.

1957—Vietcong attack South Vietnamese installations.

1962—*Feb. 6:* Major buildup of U.S. forces begins.

1964—*Aug. 7:* Gulf of Tonkin Resolution allows use of military force.

1965—*March 2:* Operation Rolling Thunder begins.

1966—*May 1:* U.S. forces hit Vietcong targets in Cambodia.

1968—*Jan. 30:* Tet offensive shakes U.S. confidence.

1969—*April 30:* U.S. troop strength in Vietnam climbs to high of 543,300.

   June 8: President Nixon begins Vietnamization; withdraws 25,000 troops.

   Nov. 15: 250,000 antiwar protesters march in Washington, D.C.

1970—*Feb. 20:* Secret peace talks open in Paris. U.S. troop strength dips as Nixon speeds up withdrawals.

1973—*Jan. 27:* Paris Peace Accord ends active U.S. role.

1975—*April 29–30:* Last Americans are airlifted from Vietnam. Saigon falls.

1982—*Nov. 11:* Vietnam Veterans Memorial dedicated in Washington, D.C.

The Tonkin Gulf Incident

In the best of all possible worlds, nations would live in peace. If conflicts arose, governments would resolve them quietly and calmly. No country would take up arms to impose its will on its neighbors.

In 1915, World War I was called "the war to end all wars." Twenty years later, World War II brought even greater horrors to our planet. Peace returned in 1945, but the world soon faced a new test. The Soviet Union was determined to spread its Communist system across the globe.

To build support for meeting the Soviet challenge, American presidents cited the "domino theory." If Communists take over one country, they warned, nearby

▲ The Gulf of Tonkin is part of the South China Sea. It is here that attacks on American naval destroyers would later lead to the Tonkin Gulf Resolution, which fell just short of declaring war on North Vietnam in 1964.

nations will "topple like a row of dominoes."[1] They too would fall to Communist forces. Sometimes this conflict was fought with words at the United Nations. At other times, bombs and bullets did the talking. In 1950, President Harry Truman sent troops to help South Korea repel an attack by North Korea. The Korean War raged for three long years before peace was restored.

In the late 1950s, a new threat arose in Southeast Asia. The Communist Vietminh had opened the conflict by driving the French out of North Vietnam (then known as French Indochina). The French had ruled Vietnam as an overseas colony since the mid-nineteenth century. Now the Vietminh were threatening the United States-backed government of South Vietnam. The danger seemed clear to the United States. If South Vietnam fell, Cambodia, Laos, and Thailand might be the next dominos to fall.

▷ A Cold War Turns Hot

In August 1964, the United States jumped into a more active role in the struggle for Vietnam. The USS *Maddox* was cruising the east coast of North Vietnam on the Gulf of Tonkin, collecting data about North Vietnamese defenses. In pursuit of that mission, the destroyer sailed within a few miles of the coast. On shore, North Vietnamese watchers were on full alert. A few nights earlier, South Vietnamese commandos had raided two nearby islands.

The *Maddox* was ready for trouble. When radar spotted three North Vietnamese torpedo boats, the crew took up battle stations. Captain John Herrick radioed for air cover and opened fire with his five-inch guns. As they closed in, the attackers launched their torpedoes. All of them missed. Moments later, a shell from the *Maddox* took out one of the torpedo boats. Jets from a U.S. Navy aircraft carrier took care of the other two.[2]

The USS *C. Turner Joy* arrived a day later to back up the *Maddox*. On the night of August 4, alarm bells rang as jumpy sailors scanned their radar and sonar screens. A seaman called out that enemy ships were heading their way. Lookouts joined in with reports that they had spotted torpedoes speeding through the water. The *Maddox* and the *C. Turner Joy* opened fire.

Crusader jets roared in to help, but no one could find the ghostly torpedo boats. Navy pilot James Stockdale later said that there was "not a ship, . . . not a wake" where the enemy should have been. A review of the action found that the young sonar man had misread his screen. Freak weather conditions may have misled the radar operators. In his report, Herrick wrote, "Entire action leaves many doubts."[3]

The USS Maddox *was the target of North Vietnamese torpedo boats on August 2, 1964. Known as the Gulf of Tonkin incident, this confrontation led to a major escalation of the conflict in Vietnam.*

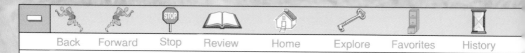
▶ Tonkin Gulf Resolution

News of the "new aggression" jangled nerves in Washington, D.C. At the White House, President Lyndon B. Johnson was gearing up for the fall election. The American people, he believed, wanted him to stand up to the Communists. After reading the Tonkin Gulf reports, he gave orders to bomb North Vietnamese patrol boat bases and oil storage facilities. Then he went on television to tell the nation that he was replying to "acts of violence."

In private, Johnson doubted that the August 4 attacks had taken place. He told an aide, "those dumb stupid sailors were just shooting at flying fish."[4] Those doubts did not keep him from asking Congress to approve the use of force. Prodded by Johnson and alarmed by news reports, Congress passed the Tonkin Gulf Resolution on August 7. Only two senators voted "no." The resolution gave Johnson the right "to take all necessary measures to repel any armed attack against the forces of the United States and to prevent further aggression."[5]

The American people cheered their government's firm stance. On election day that November, they gave Johnson an easy victory. Everyone seemed to agree that South Vietnam must not fall into Communist hands. If that happened, Laos and Cambodia would be next. After that, it might be the Philippines, even Hawaii.[6]

Driven by those fears, Johnson agreed to send more aid to the shaky government in Saigon, the capital of South Vietnam. Step by step, the nation was being pulled into a long and savage war.

The Road to War

The road that led to the Vietnam War was full of twists and turns. To a great extent, the war grew out of the clash of three forces: colonialism, nationalism, and communism. Each played a role in the power struggle that rocked Southeast Asia after World War II.

Colonialism is the practice that allows a strong nation to exploit a less-developed land and its people. Just as Great Britain once ruled its American colonies, France carved out colonies in the Far East. As a rule, the great powers took far more from their colonies than they gave. Colonial rule, in turn, inspired in captive peoples a deep love of their homeland—a concept known as nationalism. As this spirit grew, patriots took up arms against their colonial masters.

In modern times, many nationalists embraced communism as the wave of the future. In theory, communism outlaws ownership of private property. Everyone is equal, and power belongs to the workers. In practice, "rule by the workers" soon turns into rule by Communist Party leaders. Those who challenge their power often end up dead or in jail. A fiery Communist named Ho Chi Minh led the fight against colonialism in Vietnam.

▶ A Clash of Iron Wills

Vietnam shares the peninsula of Indochina with Laos, Cambodia, and Thailand. Even in ancient times, the Vietnamese wanted to be independent. Each time China conquered the region, the people found a way to break free. In the mid-1800s, the French added Vietnam to

France and the Vietminh engaged in the Indochina War from 1946 to 1954. Shown here is a squad of French legionnaires who fought in Vietnam in 1954.

their colonial empire. The Vietnamese resisted, but native soldiers were no match for troops armed with modern weapons.

French planters moved in and reaped huge profits from Vietnam's rice, rubber, and iron. In theory, they believed in liberty, equality, and brotherhood. In practice, however, they denied those rights to the people of Vietnam. Overseers treated the peasants who worked the fields and mines like slaves.[1]

Ho Chi Minh left Vietnam in 1912 at age twenty-two. He traveled to Europe, Africa, and the United States, but never forgot his homeland. After World War I, Ho begged the United States and the other Allied countries to give Vietnam its freedom. When the great powers ignored him, he became a devoted Communist. Ho returned to Vietnam after the Japanese overran Indochina during World War II. There he led a resistance movement known as the Vietminh.

At the end of World War II in 1945, Japan surrendered to the United States and its allies. Seeing an opportunity to seize the power that the Japanese had lost, the Vietminh proclaimed the Republic of Vietnam. The action angered the French, who were planning to reclaim their old colonies. Ho refused to back down. "You can kill ten of my men for every one I kill of yours," he told the French. "But even at those odds, you will lose and I will win."[2]

A Guerrilla War Takes Shape

The French ignored Ho's warning. When they returned to Vietnam, their troops ran into Vietminh resistance. It was time, the French commander said, to "teach the Viets a lesson." On November 23, 1946, a column of soldiers swept into the port city of Haiphong. French planes supplied air cover, and a cruiser turned its big guns on the city. When the soldiers pulled out, six thousand Vietnamese lay dead.[3]

The bloody "lesson" taught the Vietminh that they would have to switch tactics if they hoped to beat the well-equipped French. After blowing up a power plant in Hanoi, Ho and his followers fled into the jungle. From that day on, the Vietminh kept to the backcountry. If they had continued to challenge the French in open combat, they would have lost. Instead, General Vo Nguyen Giap trained his forty thousand men to fight a guerrilla war. Using the jungle as cover, small units ambushed French patrols and cut supply lines. When the French tried to track them down, the Vietminh seemed to vanish. Villagers fed the rebels and hid them. Many sent their sons to fight beside them.

China and the Soviet Union funneled supplies and guns to the Vietminh. Month by month, the guerrillas gained in confidence and firepower. The balance shifted again after Communist North Korea invaded Democratic South Korea in 1950. The attack, coupled with the 1949 Communist takeover in China, alarmed the United States. Was all of Asia about to be overrun? Along with sending

▲ *Ho Chi Minh, second from the right, begged western powers for Vietnam's independence prior to his takeover in 1945. At that time, no one thought that this durable leader would be celebrating the twenty-first anniversary of North Vietnam on August 22, 1966.*

troops to fight in Korea, President Harry S Truman backed the French in Vietnam. The first United States arms shipments arrived in Vietnam in June 1950. By 1954, the price tag for this aid would climb to $3 billion.[4]

General Henri Navarre took command of the French forces in May 1953. He saw at once that his troops could not win a guerrilla war. His by-the-book solution was to crush the Vietminh in a single large-scale battle. As a site for the showdown, Navarre picked a village in the northwest corner of Vietnam. Dien Bien Phu, the maps showed, lay in a long, narrow valley some 10.6 miles long and 4.3 miles wide. Forested hills that rose as high as 4,265 feet ringed the fertile valley.

Navarre was well aware of the problems his forces would face at Dien Bien Phu. Once they had occupied the valley, the French would be forced to bring in all of their supplies by air. If bad weather or enemy fire closed down the valley's airstrip, the troops on the ground would soon run out of food and ammunition. Navarre felt that the risk was worth taking. Winning a major battle in this distant corner of Vietnam, he believed, would safeguard the remaining French interests in Southeast Asia.

In January 1954, the commanding officer at Dien Bien Phu summed up the plan. "If he [the Vietminh] comes down, we've got him," Colonel Christian de Castries told his men. "And we shall at last have . . . [a] target that we can smash."[5]

Chapter 3 ▶

A Growing Commitment, 1954–1961

History books list the Battle of Dien Bien Phu as "one of the major battles of the Twentieth Century."[1] As often happens in war, the first stages of the battle drew little notice. French troops met only light resistance when they stormed the village in November 1953. Work crews quickly enlarged the small airstrip so that cargo planes could land.

Colonel de Castries ignored the hills that overlooked the base. His job, after all, was to tempt the Vietminh into launching an all-out assault. Asked about the threat of artillery fire, de Castries waved off the question. Like General Navarre, he was convinced that the Communists could not move heavy guns to this remote outpost.[2]

French planners guessed that the military post would face a single Vietminh division. General Giap had other ideas. By spring, he had slipped four combat divisions into position. To supply the troops, peasant workers cleared a narrow road through the jungle. Thanks to their labors, Giap's gunners were equipped with 180 howitzers, mortars, and antiaircraft guns.[3]

▶ Closing the Noose

French patrols were soon drawing fire each time they ventured into the hills. By mid-February 1954, de Castries had lost nearly a thousand men. After that, he kept his troops close to home. Navarre tried to even the odds by flying in fresh soldiers. Vietminh antiaircraft fire downed several transports, but others landed safely. Even so, Giap's army still outnumbered the French three-to-one.[4]

On March 13, Vietminh gunners hit Dien Bien Phu with a murderous artillery barrage. The French fought back fiercely, but they were outgunned. To make matters worse,

▲ A map of Vietnam and Southeast Asia at the time of the Vietnam War.

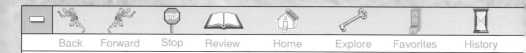
monsoon rains made airdrops risky. Little by little, the Vietminh tightened the trap. By May, the French position had been reduced to the size of a baseball field. With all hope lost, de Castries asked for a cease-fire. On May 7, the victors marched in and raised Ho's red flag over the village.[5]

▶ Vietnam Divided

Ho Chi Minh thought the Vietminh had won the right to rule all of Vietnam. Instead, the country's future was decided at a meeting far away in Geneva, Switzerland. The diplomats who met in Geneva divided Vietnam at the 17th parallel. Ho and the Vietminh were allowed to keep

▲ Bao Dai was Vietnam's last emperor, having taken the throne in 1932. After cooperating with the Japanese occupation during World War II, he stepped down when Ho Chi Minh came to power. Dai then returned to lead South Vietnam in 1954.

Ngo Dinh Diem was killed in a 1963 coup by some of his generals after having controlled South Vietnam since 1955. It is believed that his harsh policies toward Buddhists and his refusal to establish land reforms actually increased public support for Ho Chi Minh.

their grip on North Vietnam. Bao Dai, the former emperor, was picked to rule South Vietnam. In two years, the people would be asked to elect a single government for all of Vietnam.[6]

In the last days of Dien Bien Phu, President Dwight D. Eisenhower had refused to send United States troops to aid the French. Now he worried that South Vietnam would be the next "domino" to fall. To prop up Bao Dai's regime, Eisenhower increased the flow of aid. A year later, Prime Minister Ngo Dinh Diem arranged a vote that created the Republic of Vietnam. Diem, to no one's surprise, emerged as the first president. The United States showed its approval by stepping up its aid shipments.

All of Vietnam faced a major rebuilding job. Towns and cities lay in ruins. Refugees crowded the roads, most of them headed south. The North had long been the industrial heart of Vietnam. The South, thanks to the fertile Mekong Delta, had been the "rice bowl." With Ho and Diem calling the shots, both governments ruled with an iron hand. In the North, the Communists abolished private ownership of property. Anyone who protested Ho's policies was jailed or

shot. In the South, Diem was almost as tough on those who opposed him. A Catholic himself, he cracked down hard on Buddhist groups that he viewed as a threat.[7] He also refused to schedule a vote on the question of uniting the two Vietnams.

Rise of the Vietcong

Diem soon found himself facing a truly ruthless foe. In 1957, the National Liberation Front (better known as the Vietcong, or VC) emerged from hiding. These hard-line Communist rebels employed the same tactics Ho had used to defeat the French. Their first step was to turn South Vietnam's villagers against Diem. The fact that the farmers had little love for the government in Saigon simplified the task. The second step was to open a new guerrilla war. The Vietcong began by ambushing police patrols and shooting local officials. Next, they added United States advisors to their target list. In October 1957, a VC bomb wounded thirteen Americans at an office in Saigon.[8]

Until 1959, the Vietminh were busy with their own affairs. Once his power was secure, Ho resolved to "liberate" the South. Giap's People's Army of Vietnam (PAVN) sent men, guns, and supplies to the Vietcong. The shipments moved along a route known as the Ho Chi Minh Trail. The trail started in North Vietnam, crossed into Laos, and ended in South Vietnam. Dense jungles made the narrow roadway hard to spot from the air. In the early days, thousands of porters carried the heavy loads on their backs. Later, as the war grew more intense, truck convoys kept supplies moving.[9]

United States Pledges to "Pay Any Price"

For a time, the United States downplayed the Vietcong threat. The turning point came in 1961, when President

President Dwight D. Eisenhower ▶ *restricted United States involvement in the battle between North and South Vietnam because he did not want to see American troops bogged down in a land war in Southeast Asia.*

John F. Kennedy moved into the White House. The young president was a firm believer in the domino theory. If that meant sending United States troops to South Vietnam, that price would be paid.

Truman had started with thirty-five military advisors. Eisenhower had added five hundred more. Kennedy upped the count to sixteen thousand. At first, the advisors' sole job was to train the Army of the Republic of Vietnam (ARVN). Before long, the Americans were shooting back when they came under fire.[10]

The slow growth of United States involvement aroused little concern at home. Most Americans approved any steps taken to "contain" Communism. Since 1945, that policy had saved Greece, Turkey, and South Korea from Communist takeovers. President Kennedy summed up the nation's mood when he gave his inaugural address in January 1961. The United States, he said, would "pay any price, . . . to assure the survival and success of liberty."[11] No one could have imagined how high that price would be.

Chapter 4 ▶

The War Heats Up, 1962–1965

For the American people, fighting World War II made perfect sense. The Japanese attack on Pearl Harbor in 1941 united the nation in an all-out war effort. In Southeast Asia, the United States found itself in a far different kind of war.

President Lyndon Johnson, who became president after the assassination of John F. Kennedy in 1963, did not think the nation would support a full-scale war in Vietnam. Instead, he chose to wage a limited war. In the early days, this meant giving South Vietnam the support it needed to combat the Vietcong. Only the Air Force was allowed to carry the war to the North. The bombing raids were designed to cut off the flow of men and supplies to the guerrillas.

To Johnson, the Vietcong were little better than outlaws. The Vietcong thought otherwise. When they entered a village, they urged the people to join their struggle against tyranny. The call to arms often kindled a patriotic spirit that tended to overlook the dangers that lay ahead. Vietminh soldiers who marched south to fight beside the Vietcong knew better. Many wore a tattoo that read, "Born in the north to die in the south."[1]

▶ Rule and Misrule in South Vietnam

Ngo Dinh Diem badly needed his people's loyalty. Instead, his strong-arm methods divided the nation. First, his crackdown on defiant Buddhist sects stirred up religious strife. Next, he threw away the good will of much of

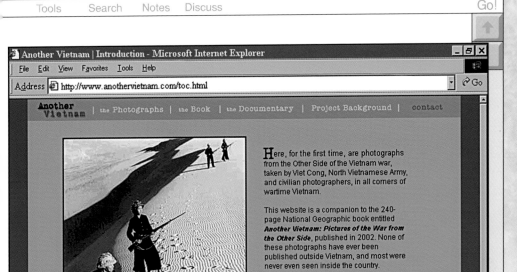

Another Vietnam | Introduction - Microsoft Internet Explorer

File   Edit   View   Favorites   Tools   Help

Address http://www.anothervietnam.com/toc.html   Go

Another Vietnam | the Photographs | the Book | the Documentary | Project Background | contact

Here, for the first time, are photographs from the Other Side of the Vietnam war, taken by Viet Cong, North Vietnamese Army, and civilian photographers, in all corners of wartime Vietnam.

This website is a companion to the 240-page National Geographic book entitled *Another Vietnam: Pictures of the War from the Other Side*, published in 2002. None of these photographs have ever been published outside Vietnam, and most were never even seen inside the country.

Altogether this book project was the culmination of more than five years' work, locating ex-war photographers, printing and scanning old negatives, and meeting with Communist bureaucrats.

By clicking on the many images here you will be able to get a glimpse of what the war looked and felt like on the other side...

Doug Niven, Editor

click to enlarge

Internet

These North Vietnamese soldiers pose for a propaganda photo on a beach just north of the demilitarized zone (DMZ).

the rural population. For centuries, villagers had voted for the councils that managed local affairs. Diem disbanded the councils because he could not control them. In their place he installed outsiders who knew little about village matters. Any loyalty he might have inspired in the countryside soon faded. Diem further angered his people by using his power to enrich himself and his friends.

Day by day, the Vietcong became more daring. Roving bands killed or kidnapped thousands of government supporters. The attacks made Diem even more ruthless. Reforms could come later, he argued.[2] As the stories of his misrule spread, the United States lost faith in him. Early in

1963, a White House advisor told some ARVN generals that the United States would welcome a change at the top.

Diem took his final misstep when he sent his police to raid a number of Buddhist pagodas. To protest the raids, a monk burned himself to death in a public square. Diem's sister-in-law, Madame Nhu, was quoted as calling the monk's death a "barbecue."[3] Her careless remarks made the Diem regime seem barbaric and uncaring. On November 1, the generals arrested Diem and his brother. A few hours later both men were dead.

Months passed as general after general tried—and failed—to govern the country. In the summer of 1965, two young officers restored order. For a time, Air Marshal Nguyen Cao Ky and General Nguyen Van Thieu ruled in tandem. Ky was flashy, while Thieu was a quiet loner. In the end, it was the cautious Thieu who emerged as South Vietnam's new strong man.[4]

The Fighting Escalates

On Christmas Eve, 1964, a Vietcong bomb exploded at a hotel in Saigon. Two Americans were killed and dozens of Americans and Vietnamese were injured. Comedian Bob Hope, the bomb's main target, was late in reaching the hotel that day. Hope did not let the close call keep him from joking with United States troops. "When I landed at Tan Son Nhut [Airport]," he told his audience, "I saw a hotel go by."[5]

In February 1965, a mortar attack on the United States base at Pleiku killed eight Americans. The attack ended President Johnson's belief in fighting a limited war. "I have had enough of this," he told his advisors.[6] Within the week he approved a series of air raids on North Vietnam. Operation Rolling Thunder hit bridges, rail lines, and missile sites. These raids followed the attack on fuel stores and power plants that followed the Gulf of Tonkin incident in 1964.

Operation Ranch Hand was already in full swing. Starting in 1962, United States and ARVN planes sprayed the forests of South Vietnam and Laos with 19 million gallons of herbicides. The plant-killing chemicals withered crops and destroyed the forest cover that concealed the Vietcong. The operation ended in 1971 amid charges that it was a form of chemical warfare. An herbicide called Agent Orange drew much of the criticism. Scientists have blamed it for causing birth defects, cancer, and other health problems.[7]

In February 1965, following a mortar attack on an American base at Pleiku, President Lyndon B. Johnson ordered a series of air raids on North Vietnam, known as Operation Rolling Thunder. He is shown here greeting American troops in Vietnam one year later.

◁ This B-66, flanked by four F-105 Thunder Chief fighter bombers, drops its bomb load on Vietcong strongholds in South Vietnam.

North Vietnam seemed to grow stronger despite the raids. The Soviet Union and China stepped up their shipments of trucks, planes, guns, and SAM (surface to air) missiles. In the South, 100,000 part-time guerrillas backed up the Vietcong's 40,000 main force troops. In combat, VC units killed ARVN troops faster than recruits could be trained. As their strength increased, the Communists stepped up their attacks.[8]

Half a world away, Americans were realizing that victory in South Vietnam would be difficult. Johnson warned that the war "will get worse before it gets better." The time will come, he said, when up to 125,000 troops would be needed.[9] In the end, his guess fell far short of the mark. In April 1968, U.S. troop strength in Vietnam topped out at 543,482.[10]

▷ **Antiwar Protests Pick Up Steam**

Johnson's remarks added to a growing national debate about Vietnam. An antiwar movement took root as draft boards inducted more men into the army. At first, the United States policy on Vietnam had been driven by "hawks" who favored the war. Now, with costs in lives and dollars rising, antiwar "doves" were speaking out. Many were college students. "We have problems to solve here at home," they said. "Why are we fighting in Vietnam?"[11]

The antiwar movement grew rapidly. Protests attracted crowds of all ages, but especially young adults. In April 1965, a student-led rally in Washington, D.C., drew twenty-five thousand protesters. College students jammed classrooms to debate the war at "teach-ins" led by their professors. Many young men burned their draft cards. Others fled to Canada to escape the draft. Buttons that read, "Make love, not war!" were hot sellers.

Protesters marched on the White House. Inside, Johnson could hear them clearly. "Hey, hey, LBJ, how many kids did you kill today?" they chanted. The president struck back by sending FBI agents to disrupt the antiwar groups. Opinion polls showed that most Americans still backed his policies. To counter the Vietcong's growing strength, he dispatched more combat troops to Vietnam.

▲ *Antiwar sentiment in the United States reached an all-time high during the Vietnam War. Here a protester offers a military police officer a flower while demonstrating against the war.*

The Turning Point, 1966–1970

As 1965 drew to a close, President Johnson felt trapped. He had poured men and money into Vietnam, only to see the Communists step up their attacks. At home, the antiwar movement was gaining vigor. In hopes of getting peace talks started, Johnson called for a Christmas pause in the bombing. Ho Chi Minh refused to take the bait. With

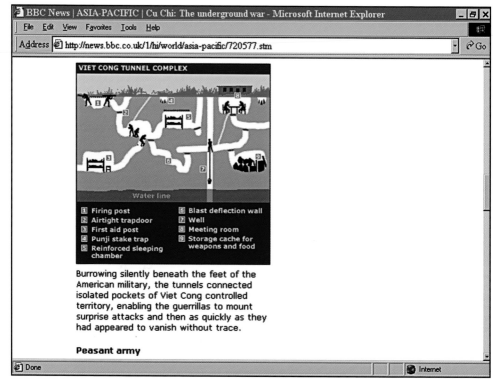

BBC News | ASIA-PACIFIC | Cu Chi: The underground war - Microsoft Internet Explorer

File Edit View Favorites Tools Help

Address http://news.bbc.co.uk/1/hi/world/asia-pacific/720577.stm   Go

VIET CONG TUNNEL COMPLEX

Water line

1 Firing post
2 Airtight trapdoor
3 First aid post
4 Punji stake trap
5 Reinforced sleeping chamber
6 Blast deflection wall
7 Well
8 Meeting room
9 Storage cache for weapons and food

Burrowing silently beneath the feet of the American military, the tunnels connected isolated pockets of Viet Cong controlled territory, enabling the guerrillas to mount surprise attacks and then as quickly as they had appeared to vanish without trace.

Peasant army

Done   Internet

▲ *Beneath the jungles of South Vietnam lies a network of tunnels, called Cu Chi, that was used by the Vietcong in guerrilla warfare against American troops. These tunnels were first built in 1948, during the war for independence from France.*

The Vietnam War - Microsoft Internet Explorer

File   Edit   View   Favorites   Tools   Help

Address http://www.vietnampix.com/fire4.htm

THE VIETNAM WAR   UNDER FIRE

BACKGROUND   MACHINES   FACES   HIPPIES   UNDER FIRE   LIFE & SORROW

A patrol of US soldiers from the 9th Division in a leech infested rice paddy field in the Tan An Delta, Vietnam, 1968.

The rice paddies with their quilt like patterns of water filled fields made movement difficult and were commonly used to set **booby traps**, particularly on the paths along the edges. The elephant grass surrounding the fields was difficult to get through and was high enough and thick enough to hide an entire military unit waiting to make an ambush.

Internet

▲ American soldiers spent long, tense hours slogging through Vietnam's muddy rice paddies. Each step took them closer to a possible Vietcong ambush or a hidden booby trap.

his "peace offensive" stalled, Johnson renewed the B-52 (heavy bombers) raids on the North.[1]

In the South, the ground war also entered a new phase. General William Westmoreland, the U.S. commander, argued that his job was to kill as many Communists as possible. In pursuit of that goal, he sent his grunts (the nickname for United States troops) on "search-and-destroy" missions. Patrols were told to seek out and attack enemy forces wherever they found them.

Quite often, the patrols could not find their elusive targets. When the Vietcong did stand and fight, they opened

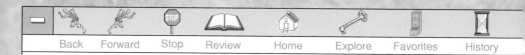

up with machine guns, mortars, and rocket-propelled grenades. When ordered to fall back, the guerrillas sowed the rice paddies with booby traps. Advancing troops had to dodge snipers, buried mines, and mortar shells tied to trees. One misstep could drop a soldier into a pit lined with sharp bamboo stakes.

To measure the success of these missions, Westmoreland's staff issued "body counts." A four-day battle in the Ia Drang valley, for example, produced what analysts called "a good kill ratio." The count was 1,300 VC dead— at a cost of 230 American lives.[2]

In 1967, Operation Cedar Falls ran up a body count of three thousand guerrillas. The operation began by forcing villagers to leave the "iron triangle" northwest of Saigon. Then the assault force blasted Vietcong strongpoints with bombs and artillery fire. To finish the job, the grunts leveled four of the largest villages with bulldozers. As a U.S. major said about a later action, "It became necessary to destroy the town to save it."[3] Leveling the buildings, it seemed, was the only way to rid the area of the Vietcong.

▷ The Tet Offensive

In November 1967, Westmoreland was feeling confident. United States casualties were high, but enemy losses were higher. He told a reporter, "I hope they [the VC] try something, because we are looking for a fight."[4] Two months later, during the Lunar New Year holiday known as Tet, the general got his wish.

Six months of planning went into the Tet offensive. General Giap's first step was to divert attention from his main targets. An assault force handled that job by hitting the United States base at Khe Sanh with artillery and rockets. The Air Force slowed the Communist thrust with

In 1968, the Tet offensive ▷ *brought Saigon under attack as Vietcong assault teams occupied large sections of the city.*

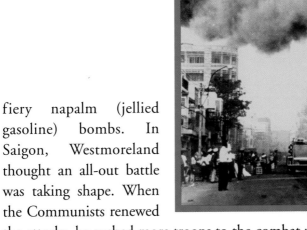

fiery napalm (jellied gasoline) bombs. In Saigon, Westmoreland thought an all-out battle was taking shape. When the Communists renewed the attacks, he rushed more troops to the combat zone.

With the United States focused on Khe Sanh, Giap launched the main Tet offensive. On January 31, 1968, ARVN troops were enjoying a New Year's cease-fire. The lull ended in the predawn hours. Some eighty-four thousand VC soldiers struck dozens of South Vietnamese cities. In Saigon, assault teams blasted their way into the American embassy. The guards had to call in airborne troops to drive them out. At the ancient capital of Hue, the guerrillas overwhelmed the defenders. Once they gained control, the VC rounded up anyone whose name appeared on their list of enemies. A relief force later found at least 2,800 bodies in a mass grave.[5]

Stung by the setbacks, United States and ARVN troops battled their way back. Foot soldiers fought house-to-house to recapture the Cholon section of Saigon. The fighting in other sectors dragged on, but the VC ran out of steam

The Vietnam War - Microsoft Internet Explorer

File   Edit   View   Favorites   Tools   Help

Address http://www.vietnampix.com/hippie3.htm   Go

Continue >>

Internet

▲ *Soldiers often used their helmets to express their opinions. This member of the 8th regiment wrote "HIPPIE" on his.*

after Hue was recaptured. By then, the guerrillas had lost forty-five thousand of their best men. American losses stood at 1,536, and ARVN units buried 2,788 dead. The brutal fighting also killed or wounded thousands of civilians.[6] Westmoreland studied the body count and claimed a hard-earned victory.

A Battlefield Victory Becomes a Political Defeat

By most measures, the general was right. The VC had little to show for the mauling they had taken. They had hoped the offensive would lead to uprisings against Diem, but those hopes died quickly. For better or worse, most city residents preferred their own flawed system.

In the United States, the Tet offensive rang alarm bells. No longer could the hawks claim "there is light at the end of the tunnel." As the *Wall Street Journal* put it, "The whole Vietnam effort may be doomed."[7] Even President Johnson was shaken. This was an election year. His hopes for winning a new term hinged on his handling of the war.

Events moved quickly in the weeks after Tet. Annoyed by Westmoreland's pleas for more troops, the White House replaced him. Then, as his public support dipped to new lows, Johnson dropped out of the presidential race. He also halted most air attacks on North Vietnam and called for peace talks. The talks opened in Paris that April, but made little headway. In the jungles and swamps of Vietnam, United States losses mounted. In 1968 alone, the war claimed 14,589 American lives.[8]

Richard M. Nixon won the White House in 1968. Once in office, he faced the same problems that had kept Johnson awake at night. Even so, Nixon believed he could "end the war and win the peace." First, he planned to push North Vietnam to the breaking point by stepping up the air war. In addition to bombing the North, Nixon approved raids on VC bases in Cambodia.

Nixon's next step was to turn over more of the fighting to ARVN troops. This policy was known as Vietnamization. The plan sounded good, but it fell apart in the field. All too often, ARVN units broke and ran when they came under fire. Reluctant soldiers saw little reason to gamble their lives to keep a corrupt government in power. Instead of search-and-destroy, Americans joked, ARVN units went out to "search-and-evade."[9]

◀ *President Richard M. Nixon was the last president who had to deal with the Vietnam War. American involvement ended on January 27, 1973, when the Paris Peace Accords were signed.*

▶ My Lai and Kent State

As Nixon laid out his plans, two events sparked new waves of antiwar protests. The first was the My Lai massacre. In March 1968, Lieutenant William Calley, perhaps on orders from his superiors, ordered his men to round up and kill the people of the small village of My Lai. Because they blamed the villagers for aiding the Vietcong, the soldiers obeyed. More than four hundred men, women, and children died that day. The story touched off widespread protests when it leaked out in February 1970. Another wave of protests broke after Nixon sent United States troops into Cambodia. On May 4, National Guard troops were called out to police a rowdy protest at Kent State University in Ohio. Alarmed by the surging crowd, the panicky soldiers opened fire. When the smoke cleared, four students lay dead.

More and more Americans were speaking out against the war. Bombing North Vietnam, they argued, only inspired its people to make greater sacrifices. Nixon tried to revive the peace talks by withdrawing eighty-five thousand troops. Ho Chi Minh had died in 1969, but the new leaders proved to be just as stubborn. Peace, they said, could come only when the last American left Vietnam.[10]

Wrapping It Up, 1971–1975

By 1971, the antiwar movement was stronger than ever. In March, the brutal nature of the war was underlined by Lieutenant Calley's conviction for the My Lai massacre. Three months later, the *New York Times* published *The Pentagon Papers*. The secret papers revealed that the government had lied to the public about Vietnam.[1] By this time, Vietnam veterans were joining the antiwar protests. In April, a large group of "Viet vets" staged a five-day rally

▲ Combat in Vietnam was especially grueling. By 1971, morale was so low that soldiers sometimes tried to harm officers whom they blamed for leading them into dangerous situations.

in Washington, D.C. To highlight the protest, some of the vets threw their combat medals onto the Capitol steps.[2]

In Vietnam, United States troops carried on the war, but morale was sagging. Drug abuse and desertion were everyday events. Drugs were easy to find and cheap to buy. A grunt could feed a heroin habit for $2 a day.[3] Soldiers also had taken to "fragging" officers they blamed for leading their units into traps. The standard murder weapon was a live fragmentation grenade rolled into someone's tent.

The White House felt the mounting pressure to end the war. In January 1972, President Nixon revealed that peace talks had been going on in Paris. In November, the two sides hammered out a long-delayed peace plan. North Vietnam agreed to a cease-fire and the return of all American prisoners of war. In return, the United States promised to withdraw its forces from Vietnam. The Communists also won the right to keep troops in South Vietnam. Promises of increased aid won Nguyen Van Thieu's reluctant consent. The three countries signed the Paris Peace Accords on January 27, 1973.

The Convoy of Tears

On March 29, 1973, the last planeload of United States combat troops left Vietnam. Only a few thousand advisors and embassy staff stayed behind. The North Vietnamese then freed the last of the 591 Americans who survived their stay in the "Hanoi Hilton."[4] This was the soldiers' name for the dismal prison in which they were confined.

Ten months later, North and South Vietnam were at war again. South Vietnamese troops regained some ground in their initial clashes with the PAVN. The Communists, it turned out, were waiting for work crews to rebuild the Ho Chi Minh Trail. Early in 1975, with supplies moving freely, General Giap launched a major offensive. As the ARVN lines crumbled, General Thieu ordered a withdrawal from the central highlands. Rather than live under Communist rule, long lines of civilians joined the retreat. Downed bridges, enemy fire, and jungle heat turned the column into a "convoy of tears." News reports of the flight spread panic through the rest of South Vietnam.[5]

By April 20, Giap's forces were closing in on Saigon. Thieu resigned his post and fled the country. Eight days later, looters ransacked the burning city. United States

People scrambled to get to the top of the U.S. Embassy in Saigon. The lucky ones were airlifted to safety before the North Vietnamese broke through the gates.

Navy helicopters were called in to rescue thousands of Americans and South Vietnamese. The last chopper flew out of Saigon on the night of April 30. A day later, the Vietcong raised their flag over the city.[6]

The Terror Spreads

The victors began to "purify" South Vietnam. The Communists began by banning long hair and clothing popular in America and Western Europe. Soon rifle squads were executing high-ranking government officials. Lower ranking officials were sent to "re-education camps." The inmates put in long days of hard labor. Each night, guards forced them to listen to lectures on communism. Some 700,000 residents of Ho Chi Minh City (the former Saigon) were forced to move to rural areas. Many South Vietnamese fled in small boats, hoping for better lives elsewhere.

No one dared seek refuge in Cambodia. By this time, Vietnam's neighbor was in a bloody revolution. When they took power in April 1975, the Communist Khmer Rouge forced millions of city residents to move to "new villages." Hunger, overwork, disease, and mass executions ran up the death toll. By January 1977, at least 1.4 million people had died in Cambodia's "killing fields." Tens of thousands of Cambodians sought refuge in Thailand and Vietnam.[7]

Healing the Wounds

Most American wars end with victory parades. After withdrawing from Vietnam, the nation found little to celebrate. Returning veterans took off their uniforms and tried to resume their old lives. For many, it was an uphill

▲ The Vietnam Veterans Memorial is dedicated to those who fought in the Vietnam War. The Wall of Names is meant to express feelings of support and sympathy for the brave men and women who gave their lives in the war.

trek. Along with their own nightmares, Vietnam vets had to endure the taunts of the antiwar crowd.

As a nation, the United States was still adding up the price of the war. One cost could be counted in dollars— $150 billion, to be exact. For many families, a far more painful price showed up in the casualty lists. The final tally came in at 58,202 Americans killed and 303,704 wounded.[8] In addition, thousands of veterans needed medical care. Aside from the sick and injured, many veterans suffered from stress disorders or drug addictions. A growing number blamed their ills on exposure to Agent Orange. Doctors warned that the most severely disabled vets would need a lifetime of care. Thousands of Americans remain classified as Missing In Action.

As passions cooled, plans were made to build the Vietnam Veterans Memorial. From day one, the project was the subject of an angry debate. Some veterans thought that the design—a polished, black granite wall—did not pay proper tribute to their sacrifices. The protests died after the Wall was dedicated in November 1982. Day after day, hushed crowds gather in Washington to leave flowers and to read the names etched into the polished surface. These emotional visits help speed the healing process.

In 1997, the United States and Vietnam took a giant step toward resuming normal contacts. President Bill Clinton sent Florida Congressman Douglas "Pete" Peterson to Hanoi as his ambassador. The choice was as popular in Vietnam as it was at home. Peterson had spent six years as a POW, but he had outgrown his anger. It was time, the former Air Force pilot said, to build a bridge across a "river of pain."[9]

Chapter Notes

Facts Page
    1. *Casualties—US vs NVA/VC,* n.d., <http://www.rjsmith.com/kia_tbl.html> (September 26, 2002).

Chapter 1. The Tonkin Gulf Incident
    1. Stanley Karnow, *Vietnam: A History* (New York: The Viking Press, 1991), p. 24.
    2. Ibid., pp. 382–383.
    3. Maurice Isserman, *The Vietnam War: America at War* (New York: Facts on File, 1992), p. 47.
    4. Ibid., p. 48.
    5. Arthur M. Schlesinger, Jr., ed., *The Almanac of American History* (New York: Barnes & Noble Books, 1993), pp. 568–569.
    6. Isserman, p. 16.

Chapter 2. The Road to War
    1. Maurice Isserman, *The Vietnam War: America at War* (New York: Facts on File, 1992), pp. 10–11.
    2. Vietnam War Quotations, n.d., <http://www.vietnamwar.net/quotations/quotations.htm> (October 8, 2002).
    3. James S. Olson and Randy Roberts, *Where the Domino Fell: America and Vietnam, 1945 to 1990* (New York: St. Martin's Press, 1991), p. 26.
    4. Isserman, p. 14.
    5. Olson, p. 38.

Chapter 3. A Growing Commitment, 1954–1961
    1. Spencer C. Tucker, *Vietnam* (Lexington, KY: University Press of Kentucky, 1999), p. 71.
    2. James S. Olson and Randy Roberts, *Where the Domino Fell; America and Vietnam, 1945 to 1990* (New York: St. Martin's Press, 1991), p. 37–38.
    3. Tucker, pp. 73–74.
    4. Ibid., p. 73.
    5. Thomas D. Boettcher, *Vietnam: The Valor and the Sorrow* (Boston: Little, Brown and Company, 1985), p. 102.
    6. Sandra M. Wittman, "Chronology of U.S.-Vietnam Relations," *Vietnam: Yesterday & Today,* n.d., <http://serverce.oakton.edu/~wittman/chronol.htm> (September 26, 2002).
    7. John Pimlott, ed., *Vietnam: The History and the Tactics* (New York: Crescent Books, 1982), p. 31.
    8. Maurice Isserman, *The Vietnam War: America at War* (New York: Facts on File, 1992), pp. 21–22.
    9. Boettcher, pp. 259–260.
    10. Editors of Time-Life Books, *This Fabulous Century: 1960–1970.* Vol. VII (Alexandria, Va.: Time-Life Books, 1970) p. 202.
    11. Isserman, p. 24.

Chapter 4. The War Heats Up, 1962–1965
    1. Thomas D. Boettcher, *Vietnam: The Valor and the Sorrow* (Boston: Little, Brown and Company, 1985), pp. 288–289.
    2. Spencer C. Tucker, *Vietnam* (Lexington, Ky.: University Press of Kentucky, 1999), p. 100.
    3. Boettcher, p. 192.

4. Maurice Isserman, *The Vietnam War: America at War* (New York: Facts on File, 1992), p. 39.

5. Boettcher, p. 290.

6. Isserman, p. 53.

7. William A. Buckingham, Jr., "Operation Ranch Hand: Herbicides in Southeast Asia, 1961–1971," n.d., <http://cpcug.org/user/billb/ranchhand/ranchhand.html> (September 26, 2002).

8. Boettcher, pp. 292–293.

9. John Pimlott, ed., *Vietnam: The History and the Tactics* (New York: Crescent Books, 1982), pp. 38–39.

10. "In Uniform and in Country," *Vietnam War Statistics,* April 12, 1997, <http://www.no-quarter.org/html/jake.html> (September 26, 2002).

11. Isserman, p. 96.

Chapter 5. The Turning Point, 1966–1970

1. Stanley Karnow, *Vietnam: A History* (New York: The Viking Press, 1991), pp. 496–497.

2. Maurice Isserman, *The Vietnam War: America at War* (New York: Facts on File, 1992), p. 75.

3. Neil Sheehan, *A Bright Shining Lie: John Paul Vann and America in Vietnam* (New York: Random House, 1988), p. 719.

4. Spencer C. Tucker, *Vietnam* (Lexington, Ky.: University Press of Kentucky, 1999), p. 136.

5. James S. Olson and Randy Roberts, *Where the Domino Fell; America and Vietnam, 1945 to 1990* (New York: St. Martin's Press, 1991), pp. 184–185.

6. *Casualties—US vs NVA/VC,* n.d., <http://www.rjsmith.com/kia_tbl.html> (September 26, 2002).

7. Karnow, pp. 560–561.

8. Isserman, p. 109.

9. Ibid., p. 77.

10. "Vietnam War," *Encarta 98 Desk Encyclopedia* (Microsoft Corporation, 1996–97).

Chapter 6. Wrapping It Up, 1971–1975

1. James S. Olson and Randy Roberts, *Where the Domino Fell: America and Vietnam, 1945 to 1990* (New York: St. Martin's Press, 1991), p. 243.

2. Thomas D. Boettcher, *Vietnam: The Valor and the Sorrow* (Boston: Little, Brown and Company, 1985), p. 462.

3. Olson, p. 230.

4. Sandra M. Wittman, "Chronology of U.S.-Vietnam Relations," *Vietnam: Yesterday & Today,* n.d., <http://serverce.oakton.edu/~wittman/chronol.htm> (September 26, 2002).

5. "Page 47," *America in Vietnam,* n.d., <http://www.ehistory.com/vietnam/books/aiv/0047.cfm> (October, 28, 2002).

6. Maurice Isserman, *The Vietnam War: America at War* (New York: Facts on File, 1992), pp. 124–127.

7. John Pimlott, ed., *Vietnam: The History and the Tactics* (New York: Crescent Books, 1982), pp. 120, 122.

8. *Casualties—US vs NVA/VC,* n.d., <http://www.rjsmith.com/kia_tbl.html> (September 26, 2002).

9. "May 1997 Review," *POW/MIA Forum,* n.d., <http://ojc.org/powforum/review/9705rev.htm> (October 31, 2002).

Further Reading

Becker, Elizabeth. *America's Vietnam War: A Narrative History.* New York: Houghton Mifflin Company, 1992.

Calvin, Linda and Sandy Strait. *What Was It Like in Vietnam?: Honest Answers from Those Who Were There.* Unionville, N.Y.: Royal Fireworks Publishing Company, 1994.

Dubois, Muriel L. *The Vietnam Veterans Memorial.* Minnetonka, Minn.: Capstone Press, Incorporated, 2002.

Dunn, John M. *A History of U.S. Involvement.* Farmington Hills, Mich.: Gale Group, 2001.

Gay, Kathlyn and Martin K. Gay. *Vietnam War.* Brookfield, Conn.: Twenty-First Century Books, Incorporated, 1996.

Karnow, Stanley. *Vietnam: A History.* New York: The Viking Press, 1991.

Kent, Deborah. *The Vietnam War: "What Are We Fighting For?"* Hillside, N.J.: Enslow Publishers, Inc., 1994.

Isserman, Maurice. *The Vietnam War: America at War.* New York: Facts on File, 1992.

Langguth, A. J. *Our Vietnam: The War 1954–1975.* New York: Simon and Schuster, 2000.

McCormick, Anita Louise. *The Vietnam Antiwar Movement in American History.* Berkeley Heights, N.J.: Enslow Publishers, Inc., 2000.

Russell, Roberts. *Leaders and Generals.* Farmington Hills, Mich.: Gale Group, 2001.

Saenger, Diane and Bradley Steffens. *Life as a POW.* Farmington Hills, Mich.: Gale Group, 2001.

Schomp, Virginia. *Letters from the Homefront; The Vietnam War.* Tarrytown, N.Y.: Cavendish, Marshall Corporation, 2001.

Wright, David. *Vietnam War.* Austin, Tex.: Raintree Steck-Vaughn Publishers, 1995.

Index

A
Agent Orange, 29, 44
antiwar movement, 30–31, 38–40

B
Battle of Dien Bien Phu, 18–19, 20–23

C
Calley, Lt. William, 38, 39
Cambodia, 12, 14, 42
Castries, Christian de, 19, 20
China, 15, 17, 30
colonialism, 15
Communists, 15, 25, 30, 42

D
Dai, Bao, 23
de Castries, Christian, 19–20, 22
desertion, 40
Diem, Ngo Dinh, 23–24, 26–28
domino theory, 11–12
drug abuse, 40, 44

E
Eisenhower, Dwight, 23

F
French involvement, 12, 15–22, 32

G
Giap, Vo Nguyen, 17, 20–21, 24,
    34–35, 41

H
Hanoi, 17
"Hanoi Hilton," 40
Ho Chi Minh Trail, 24, 41
Hope, Bob, 28
Hue, 35–36

J
Johnson, Lyndon, 14, 26, 28–33,
    36–37

K
Kennedy, John F., 24–25, 26
Kent State, 38
Khe Sanh, 34–35
Khmer Rouge, 42
Korean War, 12, 17
Ky, Nguyen Cao, 28

L
Laos, 12, 14

M
Minh, Ho Chi, 15–18, 22–24, 32, 38
Missing In Action, 44
My Lai massacre, 37–39

N
nationalism, 15
Navarre, Henri, 18–19, 20
Nhu, Madame, 28
Nixon, Richard M., 37–38, 40

O
Operation Cedar Falls, 34
Operation Ranch Hand, 29
Operation Rolling Thunder, 28–29

P
Paris Peace Accords, 38, 40
Pentagon Papers, The, 39
Peterson, Douglas, 44
Pleiku, 28

S
Saigon, 24, 35
Saigon, fall of, 40–42
Soviet Union, 11, 17, 30

T
Tet offensive, 34–37
Thailand, 12
Thieu, Nguyen Van, 28, 41
Tonkin Gulf incident, 11–14, 29
Tonkin Gulf Resolution, 14
Truman, Harry, 12, 17–18

U
United Nations, 12
USS *C. Turner Joy*, 13
USS *Maddox*, 12–13

V
Vietcong, 24, 26, 27, 30, 31, 34,
    35–36, 37, 38, 42
Vietminh, 12, 16–17, 20–21, 22–23
Vietnam Veterans Memorial, 43–44
Vietnamization, 37

W
Westmoreland, William, 33, 34, 35, 37
World War I, 11, 16
World War II, 11, 15, 16